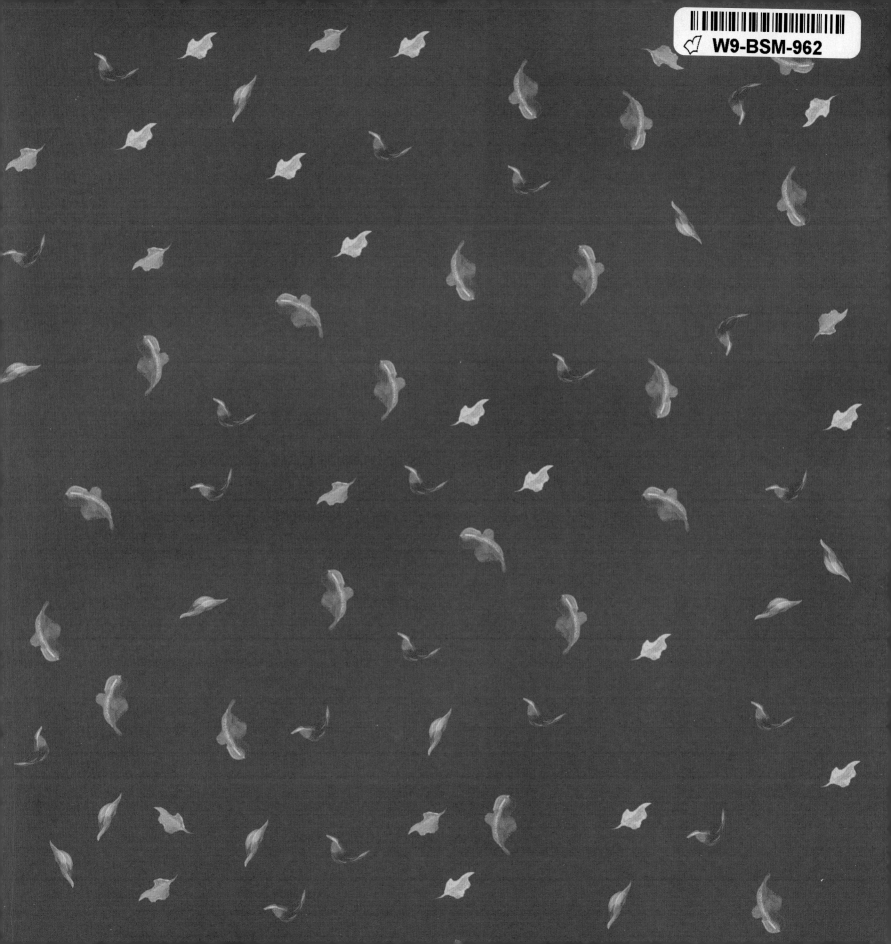

I Love You, DADDY

igloobooks

I love you, Daddy, because you
hold me up as high as the
sky and I float like a cloud.

When we walk in the woods,
you show me the way to secret places
and I follow your footprints on the path.

Daddy, I love you because you
play fun games with me and we
tumble down the hill into piles of leaves.

You kiss me tenderly and wipe
my tears away and say, "There, there,
my little bear, don't cry."

I love you, Daddy, because you say,
"Ssh," to me by the river's edge and wait for
fish to swish, so you can tickle their tummies.

You go to the honeybee tree and get
sweet honey for me and I lick my
sticky fingers and giggle.

Daddy, I love you because you pick
me up when the wild waters rush and carry
me to the safe riverbank.

You let me get muddy when we dig underground and then do it again because Mommy's not around.

I love you, Daddy, because when the summer rain falls, you splash in puddles and wipe drippy rain drops from my wet, shiny nose.

When the day is nearly done
and I'm too tired to walk,
you scoop me up and carry me home.

Daddy, I love you because you're as strong as a mountain and gentle like feathers and I'm safe in your arms, as I drift off to sleep.

I love you, Daddy, because
you're *my* daddy.